and the Terrible Tiger

Books by Geri Halliwell

Ugenia Lavender

Ugenia Lavender and the Terrible Tiger

Coming Soon

Ugenia Lavender and the Burning Pants

Ugenia Lavender: Home Alone

Ugenia Lavender and the Temple of Gloom

Ugenia Lavender: The One and Only

and the Terrible Tiger

Geri Halliwell

Illustrated by Rian Hughes

MACMILLAN CHILDREN'S BOOKS

This is a work of fiction. These stories, characters, places and events are all completely made-up, imaginary and absolutely not true.

Ugenia Lavender X

First published 2008 by Macmillan Children's Books
a division of Macmillan Publishers Limited
20 New Wharf Road, London N1 9RR
Basingstoke and Oxford
Associated companies throughout the world
www.panmacmillan.com

ISBN 978-0-230-70142-7

1 3 5 7 9 8 6 4 2

A CIP catalogue record for this book is available from
the British Library.

Printed and bound in Great Britain by MPG Books Ltd, Bodmin, Cornwall

Contents

To Bluebell. Little girl, big imagination.

1

uGenia Lavender

and the Leading Lady Thief

It was Monday morning and the sun was
beaming brightly, poking through the
curtains and giving Ugenia
a nudge that it was a
brand-new day.

Ugenia
stretched and
huffed, 'All
right, I'm
getting up!'

Then she leaped out of bed in her full Hunk Roberts, favourite action-hero way, imagining she was swinging over a shark-infested river. She dived across her room and sped to the bathroom.

As Ugenia brushed her teeth she gave herself her Extra-Special-Superstar grin in the bathroom mirror.

Today was the day when Miss Medina was going to decide who was going to get which parts in the class Golden Summer Season play.

And Ugenia was determined to be THE LEADING LADY.

It was her destiny; it was her fate; it was time to borrow her mum's nail polish and paint her fingernails shiny, metallic silver.

Ugenia's mum was a presenter on

Breakfast TV and she always looked very
glamorous and sparkling when she left for
work early in the morning, before Ugenia
was even out of bed. So it was Ugenia's
dad, who was a clever professor at the
Dinosaur Museum, who would always
be there ready with some burnt toast,
scrambled eggs and chats with Ugenia
instead.

After Ugenia's manicure, she wolfed
down her breakfast and shouted, 'Wish
me luck, Dad!' before setting off for
school.

That morning everyone was babbling
away excitedly about the play.

At break-time, Ugenia sat with Rudy,
Bronte and Trevor on their favourite bench
in the playground.

3

'I feel really inspired to give an award-winning performance,' said Rudy. 'In fact, I've already written my acceptance speech for the Oscars.'

'I've been leaping off brick walls,' said Crazy Trevor. 'Miss Medina will definitely need a stunt man and I'm ready for anything.'

Ugenia looked down at her shiny metallic silver nails as she imagined waving to a huge audience that was applauding her performance.

At that second Lara Slater entered the playground and everyone turned to stare at her.

Lara was excellent at everything; she had had the main part in last year's Golden Summer Season play and everyone had gone on and on about how brilliant she was. Ugenia tried to ignore Lara. After all, she was just an attention-seeking big show-off, right?

'Ah, Ugenia, you sweet thing. Do you want to be in the play this year?' Lara asked, smiling smugly. 'If you're really lucky perhaps you'll get to play a hedge or maybe even a dancing branch.'

Ugenia was about to say something but, at that second, Miss Medina blew her whistle and everyone stampeded towards the assembly hall, where there was going to be a special meeting about the play.

'Right,' announced Miss Medina. 'This year's Golden Summer Season play is *A Midsummer Morning's Dream* and there are two lead characters. I have already decided who is perfect to play our leading man, the zesty woodcutter. It's Will Darcy.'

The dashing Will Darcy stepped forward. Will was the class heart-throb and, as he took a long, low bow, the girls swooned and the boys groaned.

Even though Ugenia knew Darcy really liked her (he had caught what Ugenia's father called the Lovely Illness a while ago), she still felt a bit in awe of Darcy. Besides, he looked almost as dashing as Hunk Roberts, with his deep-set eyes and chiselled chin.

'However,' continued Miss Medina, 'I'm still looking for our leading lady – the Midsummer Queen.'

An electric charge of excitement crackled round the room.

'Remember,' added Miss Medina, 'it's a very big commitment and there are lots of lines to learn. There are plenty of other parts though, and bear in mind that there is no such thing as an unimportant part – it's your acting that counts!'

There were nods all round.

'So, raise your hand if you want to be our leading lady,' Miss Medina announced.

Ugenia raised her hand nervously and spotted a perfect, pointed finger sharply raised on the other side of the hall.

'Right,' Miss Medina said briskly. 'It looks like we have two contenders for our leading lady – Ugenia Lavender and Lara Slater!'

Ugenia gulped and stared at Lara's perfect, dainty nose. She pressed down nervously on her own slightly turned-up, ski-jump button nose.

'We need to find out which one of you will be our perfect Midsummer Queen,' Miss Medina continued. 'I'd like to see you both do a royal wave.'

Lara stepped forward and gave her best regal brush of the hand, and smiled her I'm-better-than-you smile at Ugenia.

Ugenia took a deep breath. She stared at Lara's beautiful, smooth blonde hair and nervously crinkled her own messy, caramel strands.

She stepped forward and gave the best royal wave she could manage.

To Ugenia's relief, Miss Medina clapped them both.

'Well done, girls,' she said, beaming. 'Now I'd like you both to read one of the queen's lines.'

She held up two scripts.

'I have the experience and the talent,' said Lara, snatching one of the scripts and giving Ugenia her I'm-MUCH-better-than-you smile.

Lara began to read in her clearest and most queenly voice.

'Oh, where are you, my darling woodcutter, on this hot midsummer morning? I'm practically melting. Release me at once from this enchanted wood.'

'Very good, Lara,' nodded Miss Medina. 'Now it's your turn, Ugenia.'

Ugenia suddenly froze as she stared at Lara's exquisite, chocolate-brown eyes and rubbed her own blue eyes anxiously.

Oh no, she thought. I'm not entirely sure how to speak like a Midsummer Queen.

But at that second, like a thunderbolt of lightning, Ugenia had a brainwave.

'INCREDIBLE!' she thought. 'I'll do it just like Queen LaLeeka in that Hunk Roberts film.'

Queen LaLeeka was the powerful and majestic leader of the distant Shero Heluka tribe and, when she spoke, all her people bowed in awe before her. Hunk Roberts had had to fight his way out of the jail the queen's monkey slaves had thrown him into.

Ugenia quickly cleared her throat.

11

'Ooooooooh, wheeeere are you, my darrrrrrling woodcutter, on this hot midsummer morning. I'm practically melting. Releeeeese me at once from this enchanted woooooooooood.'

After Ugenia had delivered her lines, three things happened.

1. There was a huge burst of applause.
2. Miss Medina cried, 'FANTASTIC!'
3. Lara glared at Ugenia.

'There's one final deciding factor,' said Miss Medina. 'I want you both to waltz with our woodcutter, Will.'

'Perfect!' exclaimed Lara. She grabbed Darcy's hand and they began to swish effortlessly around the hall. Lara gave Ugenia her biggest I'm-much-MUCH-better-than-you smile.

'Wonderful, Lara!' cooed Miss Medina. 'Now it's your turn, Ugenia.'

Ugenia stared at Lara's dainty little pink shoes, then gazed down at her own brown boots and began to feel very, very nervous.

'Go, girl!' Rudy mouthed at her.

At that second, like a thunderbolt of lightning, Ugenia had a brainwave.

'INSPIRATIONAL!' she thought. 'It's all

about acting! I'll just act as if I know how to do the waltz.'

Ugenia grabbed Darcy by the hand and took to the floor, holding her nose high in the air and pretending she was a graceful butterfly fluttering in the breeze.

'One two three, one two three,' she counted in her head. And before she knew it, she and Darcy were gliding supremely across the hall.

But Ugenia could feel a pair of steely eyes burning into her back.

They belonged to a furious-looking Lara.

Suddenly Ugenia felt her feet beginning to slip. Before she could stop herself, she and Will were tumbling through the air, finally crashing into the pianist.

A roar of laughter filled the assembly hall

as Miss Medina and the class rushed over to see if Ugenia and Darcy were hurt.

Ugenia felt so embarrassed. She closed her eyes and decided that perhaps she should pretend she was dead until everyone went home.

Finally, Ugenia opened her eyes. To her horror, Lara was peering down at her.

'Well done, Ugenia,' Lara whispered triumphantly into Ugenia's ear as Darcy limped off, rubbing his head. 'Stick to what

you're good at. I'm sure you'll make a great heap of compost!'

And with that, Lara skipped away delightedly.

A very bruised Ugenia struggled to her feet. 'I . . . I . . . I don't know what happened,' she mumbled.

'We do,' said Trevor, hurrying over to her with Rudy.

'It was Lara,' said Rudy. 'She poured some tarberry juice on the floor.'

'INJUSTICE!' cried Ugenia.

'I will put the cast list up on the noticeboard after school,' announced Miss Medina, her usual brisk self again as Ugenia, Darcy and the rest of the class composed themselves and settled back down.

☆

As soon as school finished, Ugenia, Rudy, Bronte and Trevor ran straight to the noticeboard.

'Yippee! I'm a stunt man,' yelled Crazy Trevor.

'Fabulous! I'm the wedding planner!' beamed Rudy.

'Very nice, I'm a shepherdess!' said Bronte, smiling.

Ugenia peered down the list but she couldn't see her name.

Instead she read: MIDSUMMER QUEEN, LEADING LADY: LARA SLATER

'INJUSTICE!' gasped Ugenia. 'She stole it from me!'

'Er, Ugenia,' cried Rudy, 'you have got a part!'

There, on the bottom line
of the notice, Ugenia read:

Woodcutter's son's second
cousin's alien helper – Ugenia
Lavender (AND! Understudy
to Lara Slater, the LEADING
LADY) PS Remember there are no small
parts – only small actors!!

'Woodcutter's son's second cousin's alien
helper!' groaned Ugenia. 'That's a tiny part
with only one line to say! And understudy
to the Midsummer Queen? What does that
mean?'

Lara sidled up to Ugenia. 'It means
you're my servant,' she sneered, and strutted
off down the corridor.

Ugenia felt like a crumpled piece of paper.

'That part was yours!' fumed Trevor.

'She's a cheat who stole your chance!' said Rudy.

'She's nothing but a nasty Leading Lady Thief,' said Ugenia sadly. 'Thanks for your support, guys, but I'm going home.'

Ugenia was walking very slowly down the road, dragging her heels, when someone tapped her on the shoulder.

It was Bronte.

'Ugenia, I know you're upset, but I need to tell you something.'

Bronte was one of the cleverest girls in school. She wore square black glasses and always had her nose in a book.

'Look, it's all right for you, Bronte, you got a decent part,' sighed Ugenia.

'No, you don't understand, Ugenia,' Bronte said. 'I don't want to be a snitch, but I need to tell you a secret. You know how Lara sabotaged your chance to be the leading lady today? Well, she did the same thing to me last year!'

'Really?' asked Ugenia, amazed. She hadn't known Bronte all that long but she had realized that Bronte was always much too nice to say mean things about anyone, even Lara Slater.

'She stole my costume and hid it,' Bronte explained, 'and then she locked me in the toilet.'

'INJUSTICE!' cried Ugenia furiously. 'I can't let the Leading Lady Thief get away with it again!'

☆

During the next month excitement began to grow around the school. All everyone talked about was how fantastic it was to be in *A Midsummer Morning's Dream*. All except for Ugenia, whose anger was brewing into a silent fury because she felt so cheated out of playing the Midsummer Queen.

Lara was still the leading lady. Ugenia was still the woodcutter's son's second cousin's alien helper and Lara's understudy. What was an understudy anyway? Miss Medina was so busy rushing around after Lara that there didn't seem any point in Ugenia even bothering to ask her about it.

☆

The day before the play, Ugenia still wasn't sure. Maybe I should ask my dad, she thought. After all, he is a professor and he

is very clever and he knows pretty much
everything.

So after school Ugenia jumped on her red
bike and sped down Boxmore Hill, past the
twenty-four-hour, bargain-budget,
bulk-buyers' supersized supermarket and into
the town centre. She went straight to the
Dinosaur Museum, where her dad worked.
It was an old grey building with two stone
gargoyles peering down from the roof.

Ugenia wandered through the large, stone building, under the huge diplodocus skeleton, past a stegosaurus horn, down the stairs and along a dusty, dark corridor.

She tiptoed quietly past three men in white coats wearing their do-not-disturb frowns as they peered down intently at a tiny piece of what looked like a dinosaur nostril. Ugenia knocked on her father's door, which said:

PROFESSOR
EDWARD LAVENDER
DINOSAUR CONSULTANT
—— AND ——
SPECIALIST IN PRETTY
MUCH EVERYTHING ELSE

'Enter!' called Professor Lavender.

'Hi, Dad,' said Ugenia, bursting in, 'I really need your help.'

Ugenia's father was sitting at a huge wooden desk that was covered in books, papers, maps, diagrams, pens, pencils, sketch pads, hundreds of jars of dinosaur bones, a skeleton of a baby pterodactyl, some elastic bands and eight cups of half-finished coffee.

The room was crammed with thousands of dinosaur books.

There were old books, new books, hardbacks, paperbacks, tired ones, shabby ones and some in tip-top mint condition.

'Is this about that brontosaurus we discussed at breakfast?' asked her father, giving Ugenia a kind smile.

Professor Lavender had been extremely

preoccupied with an archaeological excavation for the last month, so Ugenia hadn't had a chance to fill him in.

'No, Dad,' she said, rolling her eyes. 'It's like this.' And she told her father everything, from slipping in the tarberry juice to being Lara's understudy. 'And I don't even know what an understudy is!' Ugenia muttered. 'It's SO unfair!'

Her father thought very hard for a few moments.

'I can understand how hurtful all this is for you,' he said softly. 'You probably feel very angry, like a Tyrannosaurus rex felt when a velociraptor ate her dinner without asking.'

'That's exactly how I feel,' Ugenia replied gratefully. 'But what should I do?'

'Well,' said her father, 'in the case of the T. rex, she would crunch the raptor into sandwich spread and then eat him between two thick slices of iguanodon.'

Should I crunch Lara into sandwich spread? thought Ugenia.

'And being an understudy is actually a very important job,' Professor Lavender went on. 'An understudy has to cover the leading lady's part when the leading lady is unavailable for a performance.'

'Er, why would a leading lady be unavailable?' asked Ugenia.

Professor Lavender took off his glasses and polished them with a duster he used on archaeological dinosaur-bone-searching digs.

'Leading ladies become unavailable all the time, Ugenia,' he explained. 'Normally because they're quite temperamental, highly strung souls, who crack under the pressure of major acting roles. Either that or they get a sore throat or a sniffle or bunions or something similar.'

Suddenly, like a thunderbolt of lightning, Ugenia had a brainwave.

'Ingenious!' she gasped. 'Unavailability!'

What if Lara becomes unavailable for the play tomorrow night? Ugenia thought excitedly. Then the leading-lady part will go straight to her understudy – and that's ME!

'Thanks, Dad!' she beamed. 'You've been a great help.'

'Now would you like to see those fossilised brontosaurus droppings?' Professor Lavender called after her.

But Ugenia was already racing back down the corridor.

☆

'I have a plan!' Ugenia announced when she arrived at Rudy's. 'It's a bit of a tricky mission impossible called sabotage! I need dedication, loyalty and the best people for the job. I need you, Trevor and Bronte right away!'

Rudy quickly made a couple of calls and then pulled out a large vision board on which to write their plans. A short while later, Ugenia showed Trevor and Bronte up to Rudy's bedroom.

'Welcome to our world!' announced Rudy who was talking on two phones at the same time, scribbling on a clipboard and firing off an email on his laptop.

'Troops, take note!' declared Rudy, pointing to the vision board.

UGENIA AND RUDY'S REVENGE PLAN FOR LARA, *THE LEADING LADY THIEF*:

1. FISHY LINING: LINE LARA'S GOLDEN GOWN WITH ULTRA-FISHY FISH - PREFERABLY KIPPERS (THE STINKIER THE BETTER), THUS REPELLING DARCY AND CAUSING LARA MUCH MISERY.

2. THE GARLIC GIFT: GIVE LARA A SECRET CHOCOLATE GIFT - LIBERALLY LACED WITH GARLIC - RESULTING IN STINKY BREATH, THUS REPELLING DARCY AND CAUSING LARA EVEN MORE MISERY.

3. HEEL STREET BLUES: BREAK HEEL OF LARA'S LEFT SLIPPER, THUS REPELLING DARCY WITH HER WOBBLY DANCE MOVES AND CAUSING LARA HUGE EXTRA MISERY.

4. RASPBERRY REVENGE PUNCH: SPIKE LARA'S RASP-BERRY DRINK WITH PRUNE JUICE, MAKING THE TOILET LARA'S NEW BEST FRIEND, THUS REPELLING DARCY AND CAUSING LARA EXTRA-SPECIALLY MASSIVE MISERY.

MISERY X 4 = LARA CRACKS UNDER THE PRESSURE = UNAVAILABLE TO PLAY LEADING LADY = UGENIA BECOMES LEADING LADY

'Wow!' gasped Crazy Trevor.

'Very nice!' nodded Bronte.

☆

Ugenia, Rudy, Trevor and Bronte set to work the second they got to school the next day.

STRIKE ONE: Rudy carefully lined Lara's Midsummer Queen's golden gown with the stinky kippers his mother had thrown out that morning.

STRIKE TWO: Trevor planted the secret milk-choccy garlic gift in Lara's locker with a love note attached from Darcy (so she'd definitely eat it).

STRIKE THREE: Bronte hammered off the left heel of Lara's violet slippers.

STRIKE FOUR: Ugenia secretly poured a big helping of lethal prune juice into Lara's raspberry drink.

'Job well done!' beamed Ugenia. 'Now let's see the results. By the end of the afternoon, I will be the leading lady.'

But at the dress rehearsal things didn't quite go as planned . . .

1. Lara wore a new green gown Miss Medina had brought in because she thought it was better than the golden one.

Injustice! thought Ugenia. But there's always Strike two.

2. Lara handed Darcy the secret milk-choccy garlic gift. 'I only like dark chocolate,' she explained.

Double injustice! thought Ugenia, but there's always Strike three.

3. Lara appeared barefoot. 'My Midsummer Queen needs to feel the grass under her feet,' she said importantly.

Treble injustice! But there's always Strike four, Ugenia thought as she watched bossyboots Lara making demands of her other classmates in the play.

'Hey, Winslet! Stop flapping and pass me that hairgrip IMMEDIATELY!'

'Hey, DiCaprio, come and powder my nose!'

'And you, Darcy – pass me my raspberry drink.'

'Oops, sorry, Lara,' said Darcy, blushing. 'I drank it – I thought it was mine. Would you excuse me for a moment?'

And with that, Darcy dashed for the toilets.

Ugenia groaned. Four strikes. Four disasters!

'Right,' announced Miss Medina. 'While we wait for Will, let's have our two woodcutter's son's second cousin's alien helpers.'

There were two alien helpers – Ugenia and Henry. Henry was normally very helpful, but today he was in a foul mood as he didn't want to be an alien helper either.

Ugenia and Henry were both wearing the same spangly green egg-shaped suits.

'Let's get on with it,' muttered Henry,

scowling. 'You say your line then I'll do mine.'

'Er . . . Has earth got a dark side like me?' said Ugenia.

'WRONG!' snapped Henry. 'Get it right, you stupid girl!'

'Er . . . Has earth got a dark side like you?' tried Ugenia.

'WRONG again, you idiot!' hissed Henry.

'Stop being so horrid, Henry!' shouted Ugenia, storming off the stage and running out of the hall.

Ugenia's plan had failed and she couldn't even get her one line right – and there was no more time to practise it as they were performing that evening.

Miss Medina announced that the cast

could take a meal break but that they had
to be back and ready in one hour.

Ugenia walked slowly back to the
Dinosaur Museum, still wearing her spangly
green alien-helper outfit. She knocked sadly
on Professor Lavender's door.

'Hi, Dad,' she said meekly, 'I really need
your help.'

Quickly Ugenia told her dad everything
about the leading-lady-sabotage-plan
disaster and her failure as an alien helper.

Professor Lavender took off his glasses
and polished them with the duster he
used on archaeological dinosaur-bone-
searching digs and gave Ugenia a very
serious look.

'It sounds like it's you who has become
the Leading Lady Thief,' he said quietly.

Ugenia suddenly felt a huge dose of SHAME.

Her dad was right. She had become the Leading Lady Thief.

I've become as bad as Lara, she thought sadly.

Professor Lavender pulled open one of his desk drawers and rummaged around. He took out a pair of sparkly space-hopper antennae. 'These are original blingosaurus antennae from the museum's miscellaneous department,' he explained. 'You can borrow them for the play if you like.'

Ugenia took them and nodded gratefully. 'The best revenge in the world is success,'

said her dad, smiling as he placed the antennae on her head. 'I want you to be the best woodcutter's son's second cousin's alien helper you can be.'

'You're right, Dad,' Ugenia declared, 'I have some acting to do!'

'Now would you like to see those fossilized brontosaurus droppings?' he called after her.

But Ugenia was already racing back down the corridor.

☆

Ugenia burst into the assembly hall, grabbed Henry and dragged him straight on to the stage.

'Has earth got a dark side like US?' pronounced Ugenia proudly.

Henry stared at her in amazement.

'Wow!' he gasped. 'That was amazing, Ugenia. And I love your extra alien head-gear. You really are a great actress!'

Ugenia beamed. Henry didn't seem so horrid any more.

'There are no small parts, only small actors!' giggled Ugenia.

At that moment, Ugenia heard Miss Medina's voice.

'Ugenia!' cried the teacher. 'Lara's been taken ill.'

'Oh no,' gulped Ugenia. 'Lara must have had some of the raspberry drink after all.'

'Has she been sick?' Ugenia asked Miss Medina.

'It's not her stomach,' Miss Medina replied, frowning. 'She's lost her voice because she's been barking out so many orders. So now we need our Midsummer Queen understudy – and that means you, Ugenia!'

'Result!' cried Ugenia. 'I mean . . . I'm so sorry to hear that,' she muttered.

'Oh, and by the way – you have to wear the original gold dress as Lara has got the zipper stuck on the new green one,' Miss Medina told her.

'No problem!' smiled Ugenia, slipping on the stinky gold kipper dress and the wonky violet slippers.

'Now, Ugenia,' said Miss Medina briskly, 'all the parents will be arriving soon and the play will be starting in a short while. I know there are lots of lines for you to say, but I'm sure you've done your understudy job very well, haven't you?'

Ugenia looked at Miss Medina blankly.

'Ugenia? YOU DO KNOW THE LEADING LADY'S LINES, DON'T YOU?' Miss Medina said, suddenly looking worried.

'Lines?' gasped Ugenia. 'What lines?'

Big News!

Helloooooooo, everyone!
SOOOO?? What do you
reckon? Are you a little disappointed
with my diva-like behaviour?
Apparently a diva is someone who
throws a tantrum when she doesn't
get what she wants! And that's just
what I did for a while there, until

I realized I was behaving just as badly as Lara Slater.

I did get in a bit of a pickle, didn't I? But it all turned out fine in the end. I did manage to be the leading lady, although I had to make up the lines as I went along, which confused Will Darcy a bit. He didn't seem to mind too much though. I think his Lovely Illness hasn't worn off yet (remember my first book and the story called 'The Lovely Illness'? My dad was funny – he says that when someone really likes you, like Will Darcy likes me, he has the Lovely Illness), so he was quite nice to me,

even when I made a few mistakes
– although he did hold his nose
a bit because I stank of kippers!
So yeah, I got a massive round of
applause at the end of the play.
Everyone was quite impressed with
the way I just jumped in there
when Lara couldn't go on.

But I have to say I was really
worn out after the show. Being a
leading lady is hard work. So I'm
going to put my feet up and relax
with Rudy. His mum is making us
curry – cool!

Big X0
Ugenia Lavender XX

Ingenious Top Tip

What annoys me about you, is usually in me!

You see how bothered I was about Lara Slater's behaviour when she stole my part and turned into a Leading Lady Thief? And yet I was quite capable of being just as bad. I nearly turned into a Leading Lady Thief myself!

2

UGenia Lavender

and the Terrible Tiger

The sun was yawning and only thinking
about getting up when Ugenia jumped out
of bed.

She got washed, dressed (in her new
black and orange stripy T-shirt), packed her
lunch box and stuffed her yellow rucksack
in less than twenty seconds.

She was definitely, absolutely, READY
TO GO!

And why was she ready so quickly?

Because today was the class mystery trip, that's why!

'Is it time to go yet?' yelled Ugenia, leaping on to her parents' bed.

'Ugenia!' groaned her father. 'The school bus isn't coming for another hour!'

'Injustice!' huffed Ugenia, going downstairs and flicking on the TV in the kitchen.

She munched on some golden nutty cornflakes and sat down to watch her mum on Breakfast TV.

Ugenia liked seeing her mum asking people awkward questions, but she LOVED it when Pandora got their names wrong or made them cross.

As Ugenia turned the television on, a man with a shiny bald head (that looked like a boiled egg), and wearing a tweed jacket, was waving a big rifle in the air. He was sitting on the famous cream sofa next to her mum, ranting and raving about something.

'Blah, blah, blah,' went the man.

'BORING!' cried Ugenia.

Suddenly a golden tiger filled the screen. It was running gracefully through a huge grassy field beneath a burning sun and a crystal-clear blue sky.

'INCREDIBLE!' gasped Ugenia as she gazed at the beautiful creature.

'Hunting tigers is wonderful, Pandora,' the man on the couch grunted, to Ugenia's horror.

'But if you hunt tigers, Major Glutt,' replied Pandora with a frown, 'aren't you worried that they may become extinct?'

'Who cares if they're extinct, Pandora?' the man laughed. 'Tigers are stupid, dumb animals! And besides, if we don't hunt 'em, where would we get our tiger-skin rugs from? It's fair game, Pandora. FAIR GAME!'

'INJUSTICE!' screamed Ugenia at the television. 'You horrible murderer! I hope those tigers bite your head off! And how dare you call my mother Pandora? You don't even know her!'

She grabbed the telephone and quickly dialled 33306984554378293, the number of the TV station.

'Can I speak to Pandora Lavender,

please?' Ugenia said in her most important voice. 'It's her daughter, Ugenia Lavender.'

'I'm sorry, she's not available at the moment,' replied a voice.

'INJUSTICE!' cried Ugenia, slamming down the phone.

At that moment she heard a beep outside. It was the school bus. Of course! The class mystery trip!

Ugenia ran on to the bus and took a seat at the back, next to her best mates, Rudy, Crazy Trevor and Bronte.

'Where do you think we're going?' asked Ugenia excitedly.

The Transport Museum would be nice,' said Bronte.

'The Fashionista Department Store would be fabulous,' said Rudy.

'The Bare-Knuckle Mudbath Wrestling Arena would be magic!' said Crazy Trevor.

☆

Fifteen minutes later, the bus turned off the road and suddenly, there in front of them, was an enormous yellow and blue stripy tent.

'Very, very nice,' said Bronte.

'Fabulous!' said Rudy.

'Er . . . yeah . . . magic,' said Trevor.

A gangly man, with enormously thick
eyebrows, wobbled up to them on stilts and
declared through a megaphone: 'My name
is Sherman Barnaby Willoughby Trent. I
am your circus host and your ringmaster for
the day. Please follow me!'

Sherman Barnaby Willoughby Trent walked speedily across the car park. The children had to walk double fast to keep up as they followed him into the big top.

The big top was as big as a bank. No, make that a shopping centre. No, make that a city!

There were rows and rows of seats curving all the way round the big ring in the middle. The whole place smelt of

popcorn, toffee apples and bubblegum.

Ugenia, Rudy, Trevor, Bronte and the rest of the class sat with

Mr Lemming, the deputy head.

Suddenly, there was a loud squeal from a trumpet.

Sherman Barnaby Willoughby Trent bounded out from behind a curtain.

He was now wearing a red ringmaster's tailcoat and a shiny black top hat.

'Ladies and gentlemen, boys and girls,' he declared through his megaphone. 'Welcome to the greatest show on earth!'

And with that, the show began.

Acrobats wearing shiny green catsuits swung from the high trapeze, far above the big top's safety net.

Crazy clowns flung cream pies into each other's faces.

Knife-throwing dragon men hopped about on one-legged inflatable elephants.

Fire-eating unicorn women cartwheeled through hoops of fire.

Then the ring went completely dark.

'And last but not least,' announced Sherman through his megaphone, 'please welcome the greatest animal-lover on earth – Mr Roy Friedegg!'

Suddenly, under the glare of a shining spotlight, appeared a man with greasy white-blond hair, leather trousers (that were a bit too tight), sunglasses and a hairy chest that was poking out through his silky mauve shirt. Over the shirt he wore a sparkly leopard-skin jacket.

'It's not easy being me, but somebody's got to do it!' laughed Roy, as a second

spotlight revealed a large, golden stripy
tiger in a huge silver cage.

'Watch and learn,' said Roy, taking a
silver key from his jacket pocket, unlocking

the cage door and stepping inside.

The crowd gasped.

'I am the bravest man in the world,'
declared Roy, waving a big whip in the air
as the tiger jumped through a hoop.

The crowd gasped even louder.

Roy slashed the whip and the tiger
ran round in circles. 'I just ADORE my
precious little pussycat,' announced Roy
with a cheesy grin.

'That tiger looks amazing,' whispered
Bronte.

Roy cracked his whip again and the tiger
balanced on a chair.

'No,' whispered Ugenia, 'that tiger looks
terrible.'

'What do you mean?' whispered Rudy.

'She doesn't look like she actually enjoys

jumping through hoops, running round in circles and balancing on chairs,' replied Ugenia. 'Would you?'

Ugenia stared at the tiger and the tiger stared back at Ugenia.

Finally Roy bowed proudly and left the cage, locking the door behind him and dropping the key back into his jacket pocket.

Everybody cheered and clapped except for Ugenia, Rudy, Trevor and Bronte.

And with that, the show was over.

'That man is a disgusting bully and he does NOT love that tiger,' said Ugenia,

biting into her golden-nutty-cornflake
sandwich, as she sat on a wooden bench
having her lunch with the others.

'It's sad,' said Bronte

'It's terrible!' said Rudy.

'Er . . . yeah . . . terrible,' said Trevor.

'This is our chance to do something to
help that tiger,' said Ugenia, not actually
knowing what that something was.

'Follow me,' she said as she sneaked off
towards the back of the tent. 'We have
work to do.'

They hurried along a corridor and came
to a blue door. On it was a sign reading:

STAR PERFORMER
Mr Roy Friedegg

Ugenia knocked.

The door was yanked open. There stood Roy Friedegg and behind him was the large tiger. But now she was in a very small and rusty cage, and she looked really terrible.

'Hello, children,' grinned Roy, smoothing down his greasy, white-blond hair. 'Hope you enjoyed the show. Elsa is resting now. We have to keep her locked up. She is a very dangerous animal. We wouldn't want her to get out.'

Ugenia stared at Elsa, and Elsa stared back at Ugenia.

Ugenia suddenly saw Friedegg's sparkly leopard-skin jacket hanging on a hook on the wall. Like a thunderbolt of lightning she had a brainwave. INGENIOUS! she thought. We'll get Elsa out!

'I have a plan,' she whispered to the others when Friedegg's back was turned, and she dropped her one pound spending money on to the floor.

'Does that belong to you, sir?' asked Ugenia innocently.

Roy stared at the floor and spotted the coin. 'I believe it does,' he said, smiling.

As Roy reached down to pick up the coin, Ugenia reached up to his jacket.

'Thank you so much for finding that money,' said Roy, straightening up again.

No, thought Ugenia, thank *you* so much.

'We just want to say hello to Elsa,' said Ugenia with her sweetest, most innocent apple-pie smile.

'OK, but remember she's a terrible tiger,' warned Roy. 'Don't put your hands through the bars of the cage unless you want to be her lunch!' he laughed, wandering off to get a bite to eat.

'I think Elsa needs some time out,' said Ugenia, dangling Roy's key (the one she'd pulled out of his jacket pocket) with a smile.

'What if she scratches us?' asked Bronte.

'I'll scratch her back,' said Trevor.

'What if she bites us?' asked Rudy.

'I'll bite her back,' said Trevor.

'What if she eats us?' asked Bronte.

'Er . . . yeah . . . that would be . . . terrible,' said Trevor.

Ugenia took a deep breath.

Elsa stared at Ugenia, and Ugenia stared at Elsa.

Ugenia turned the key in the lock and the cage door swung open.

Am I making a terrible mistake? quivered Ugenia, as the tiger opened its huge mouth and flashed its giant white teeth. Am I about to become her lunch?

But to Ugenia's surprise, the tiger's teeth began to chatter.

'This tiger isn't terrible, she's terrified,' said Ugenia, stepping slowly into the cage.

The tiger began to shake even more and backed into a tiny corner of the cage. Then she started to sniff and slowly, following her nose, she crept towards Ugenia and started sniffing her rucksack.

'INCREDIBLE,' cried Ugenia. 'Elsa likes candy!'

'It's all right,' said Ugenia, reaching into her rucksack. 'Do you want a bite of my supersized caramel-fudge hard-candy lolly on a pink stick?'

The tiger took a lick of the lolly and purred. 'That's better, you adorable pussycat,' grinned Ugenia.

'I can hear someone coming!' hissed Rudy.

Ugenia slammed the cage door shut and, quick as a flash, the four of them bounded out of the room and ran all the way back to the school bus.

☆

Before she knew it, Ugenia was back home, eating spaghetti with her mum and dad in front of Prime Fast News Channel 24.

'And here's some breaking news,' said the presenter. 'A very dangerous tiger has just escaped from Barnaby's Big Top Flying Circus, seriously injuring her trainer, Mr Roy Friedegg. The ferocious tiger was last seen running towards the town centre.'

'INJURIOUS!' gulped Ugenia, 'I FORGOT TO LOCK THE CAGE DOOR!!!!!'

'If you have any information about Elsa's whereabouts please ring 44876294837162000,' said the presenter, reeling off the long telephone number.

Ugenia gulped very nervously.

'Er . . . Mum . . . Dad . . . there's something I need to tell you. It's all my fault!' And with that, Ugenia told them everything.

When she'd finished, Mum looked at Dad. Dad looked at Mum. They both looked at Ugenia.

'YOU'RE GROUNDED!' they said together. 'Go to your room.'

Ugenia decided that this was a battle she wasn't going to win, so she walked sadly up to her room in defeat.

It was karate night with Crazy Trevor, but she didn't have a hope of going.

Roy Friedegg has been seriously injured, thought Ugenia, and it's all my fault. And Elsa is out there all alone.

I'm awful, she thought as she paced to the right.

I'm terrible! she thought as she paced to the left.

Suddenly Ugenia heard a tapping sound. It was Crazy Trevor throwing pebbles at her window.

Ugenia ran to the window and threw it open.

'Your mum says you're grounded,' Crazy Trevor shouted up to her. 'Does that mean you can't come to karate?'

'Of course it means I can't come to karate. I'm grounded, you duh-brain!' growled Ugenia, who was now pacing her room frantically to the right and to the left. 'Elsa's escaped.'

'Easy, tiger,' said Trevor. 'Don't bite my head off. I was only asking.'

'I just feel so terrible about Elsa,' said Ugenia.

'She probably feels terrible too,' said Trevor. 'She's out there all alone with nothing to eat.'

'It's all my fault!' cried Ugenia, as she

felt the remains of the supersized caramel-
fudge hard-candy lolly on a pink stick in
her pocket.

'INSPIRATIONAL!' cried Ugenia. 'She
loves candy! I know exactly where to find
her! We have to rescue her, Trevor. Help
me escape from my cage.'

Ugenia threw her bed sheet down to
Trevor and he tied the sheet to four
rose-bushes.

In a flash, Ugenia leaped out of the
window and landed safely on her very own
Big Top Flying Circus safety net.

'Come on, let's go to the twenty-four-
hour, bargain-budget, bulk-buyers'
supersized supermarket, NOW!'

Ugenia jumped on the back of Crazy
Trevor's chunky blue mountain bike and

they flew down the hill as fast as a trapeze swing.

Five minutes later they arrived at their destination. They leaped off Trevor's bike and ran inside the supermarket, which was nearly empty.

Ugenia felt a bit scared as they took a trolley and pretended to do their weekly shop.

They wandered into the fresh-vegetables aisle.

There were cauliflowers and cabbages, cucumbers and carrots, but no tiger.

They wandered into the frozen-meat-and-fish aisle.

There were sausages and salami, salmon and sea bass, but no tiger.

They wandered into the confectionery-and-cakes aisle.

There were marshmallows and mints, macaroons and marzipan, but no tiger.

Or was there?

Ugenia crept forward and suddenly spotted a stripy behind,

behind the coconut-brownie display.

There was Elsa, drooling and licking a supersized caramel-fudge hard-candy lolly on a pink stick.

Ugenia looked at Elsa, and Elsa looked at Ugenia.

'Sorry to disturb your snack,' whispered Ugenia, 'but we need to get you out of here. Come on, Elsa.' And Ugenia helped the terrified tiger to climb into the shopping trolley.

Carefully avoiding being seen by the other shoppers, Ugenia quickly pushed Elsa out of the supermarket and up the hill, just as the sun was setting. Crazy Trevor wheeled his bike beside her.

'I'm taking you home,' said Ugenia to Elsa. 'Mum and Dad will know what to do.'

☆

As they arrived back at Ugenia's house, her mother, Pandora, appeared at the front door.

'Ugenia Lavender!' gasped her mum, looking terrified. 'What is THAT in your trolley? And what are you doing out of your bedroom?'

'This is Elsa, Mum,' Ugenia said soothingly. 'She needs our help. Don't worry, she's not terrible – she's just a big, gentle pussycat. And she's our new house guest!' Ugenia added, giving her sweetest and most innocent apple-pie smile.

Elsa gave Pandora a huge friendly slobbery lick as if to say thank you.

Then they went inside, and Ugenia curled up on the sofa with Elsa and told her mum everything.

☆

The next morning on Breakfast TV, Pandora, Ugenia, Elsa the tiger and Roy Friedegg (who had a large bandage on his nose) all sat squashed together on the famous cream sofas.

'Good morning,' announced Pandora brightly, 'today we have a very special guest – Ugenia Lavender, who rescued this tiger, Elsa, after she escaped from Barnaby's Big Top Flying Circus. And we also have Elsa's trainer, Mr Roy Friedegg. Tell us what happened, Roy.'

'Well, it's like this,' said Roy. 'It was a very dangerous situation and that terrible tiger bit me . . .'

Ugenia began to zone out.

'Blah blah blah,' said Roy.

'BORING!' thought Ugenia as she watched beads of sweat trickle down Roy's forehead.

Suddenly Roy's greasy, white-blond hair began to slip down his face.

'It's a toupee!' cried Ugenia.

But before Ugenia could say anything, Elsa snatched Roy's hairpiece in her mouth, revealing Roy's shiny bald head (that looked like a boiled egg), and ran to the back of the studio with it.

'GIVE ME THAT BACK YOU STUPID, DUMB ANIMAL!' shrieked Roy.

That sounds familiar, thought Ugenia.

Like a thunderbolt of lightning, Ugenia suddenly had a brainwave.

'IMPOSTER!' she screamed. 'Roy Friedegg is MAJOR GLUTT!'

Roy Friedegg/Major Glutt began to chase Elsa and Ugenia around the studio.

'Perhaps it's time to introduce our next guest – Mr Sherman Barnaby Willoughby Trent,' said Pandora, looking flustered.

A fuming Sherman appeared on the screen. 'Thank you, Ugenia, for exposing Roy Friedegg as Major Glutt – the horrible animal-hater,' said Sherman. 'I would like to apologize to Elsa. Elsa was born free and should remain that way. Oh, and by the way – Roy Friedegg or Major Glutt or whatever you call yourself – YOU'RE FIRED!'

'In fact we at Breakfast TV had a phone-in,' explained Pandora. 'Our viewers have voted that Elsa will be going to a new home at a

lovely tiger sanctuary. Do you have any comments on that, Roy Friedegg/Major Glutt? I think you're in big trouble.'

Roy Friedegg/Major Glutt was on his knees at the back of the studio, hiding behind his toupee in terrified silence.

'Nothing to say, Roy? Or has the cat got your tongue?' asked Pandora.

'I have something to say,' said Ugenia, smiling.

'It's fair game . . . Pandora. FAIR GAME!'

And Ugenia winked at the tiger, and the tiger winked back at Ugenia.

Big News!

Hi!!
Wow, did that adventure keep you on the edge of your seat or what! It did me. Maybe it should have been called the Frustrated Tiger, because – oh boy – did I feel frustrated when I saw Elsa being mistreated. And

I felt even more frustrated when I was grounded. I felt like a caged animal; it was awful.

Anyway, meeting Elsa was so cool. Now I'm allowed to visit her whenever I want – well, when Mum will let me, of course. My mum is pretty cool actually. I know sometimes she can get a bit bossy, but she means well, I suppose, and she's only doing what she thinks is best for me. That's what she tells me anyway!

So what did you think of Roy Friedegg/Major Glutt? Major idiot more like. I knew something wasn't right about him!

Anyway, he got his comeuppance, don't ya think?

You know what's lovely? My friend Trevor really showed up for me too.

Hmm, I was thinking . . . since you've been around a bit, does that mean we're becoming friends?? I hope so!

Big hug from your possible NBF (new best friend)

Ugenia Lavender XX

Ingenious Top Tip

What goes around comes around

OK, a brilliant example of this is what happened to Roy Friedegg/Major Glutt.

He was being really horrible to Elsa, so eventually people were horrible to him. His nastiness came round and bit him on the bottom!

3

uGenia Lavender

Who Do U Think U R?

Ugenia woke up with a massive smile on her face. She felt as if her heart had grown a little bit overnight. She leaped out of bed, skipped to the bathroom and gave herself an extra-big grin in the mirror, pretending she was in a toothpaste advert.

Now, why did Ugenia feel so good?

Because everything was going her way, that's why!

1. Will Darcy had caught the Lovely Illness and kept sending her soppy poems.

2. She'd got to play the leading lady in the class summer play.

3. She'd been on Breakfast TV with Elsa the tiger.

All this good stuff gave Ugenia an extra spring in her step. It was like being an Extra-Special-Superstar except without the limo and lots of staff fussing over her.

But really the best and biggest thing was that when she went to school now she felt . . .

POPULAR!!

Today, when Ugenia approached the school gates, lots of people smiled at her and said nice things.

'Hi, Ugenia!' said Sita. 'I loved your dancing in the summer play! Would you like to come to my house for tea?'

'I love your boots, they're really great!' said Sebastian.

'That was so cool with you and the tiger!' said Max. 'Wanna game of footy at lunchtime?'

'Can I have your autograph?' said Billy, looking shy.

'Wow, you were on TV!' said Chantelle. 'You can borrow my Rollerblades, if you like.'

Ugenia lapped up the attention, smiling proudly. 'Thanks, I'd love to. Sounds great! Yeah, fabulous!'

Ugenia went to each lesson feeling fabulous. It was almost as if her popularity was contagious.

'I love your hair. It's so beautiful,' said Henry.

'Can I sit next to you?' asked Liberty.

'No, she's sitting next to ME,' said Anoushka, shoving Liberty out the way.

'I said Bronte could sit there,' said Ugenia.

'Bronte, be a love and sit somewhere else?' said Anoushka, and with that Bronte

got up
quietly
and
moved.

'Sorry,
Bronte!'
said Ugenia, shrugging her shoulders.

Ugenia went to PE, where two teams
were being picked for rounders.

'Ugenia, you're on my team,' said red
team captain, Crazy Trevor.

'No, Ugenia's on MY team,' said blue
team captain, Cara, dragging Ugenia
over. 'I have my own special bat you can
borrow, Ugenia!'

'Er, OK then,' said Ugenia, shrugging
her shoulders at Trevor as if to say, 'Oops,
sorry, I can't help it.'

☆

After PE Ugenia went to lunch and was about to join her friends Rudy, Trevor and Bronte at their table, when Max slid his arm around her and guided Ugenia to his table where all *his* friends sat.

'But I was going to sit with MY friends,' muttered Ugenia.

'I'm your friend, and I have a packet of spaghetti-flavoured crisps you can have,' announced Max.

'Er, OK then,' said Ugenia, giving Rudy a look that said, 'Sorry – hope you don't mind!'

The rest of the day was much the same. In fact, the rest of the week was much the same. In fact, the rest of the month was much the same!

Wherever Ugenia went, she was always the centre of attention, everyone wanted to be her friend, and everyone said nice things to her and asked her to join in with what they were doing . . .

'Would you be captain of the netball team?'

'I really love that T-shirt you're wearing.'

'We'd like you to be a member of the Computer Club – in fact, will you officially open the new computer room for us?'

'I think the way you walk is just brilliant.'

'Will you be guest of honour at my birthday roller disco?'

☆

On Friday after school, Ugenia went to see her great-granny, Betty. Granny Betty, as Ugenia called her, lived in an old house

round the corner from Ugenia's home at
13 Cromer Road. Outside her house stood
a rusty old car that she never drove.

Granny Betty was more than just your
ordinary 101-year-old great-grandmother.
She was extraordinary!

'Granny Betty, you'll never guess what!'
gushed Ugenia.

'You've become extremely popular and
everyone wants a bit of Ugenia?'

'Yes! It's great, isn't it!' said Ugenia
proudly.

'Well, just don't get too caught up with
it all. It's important to remember who your
real friends are, and to keep them,' said
Granny Betty.

'Yeah, all right, Gran, I'm just enjoying
all this attention for once. I've wanted to be

the cool one in class for so long and now it's happening!' explained Ugenia as she helped herself to some of Granny Betty's ultra-yummy Christmas cake, even though it was summer.

(Granny Betty treated every day like it was Christmas even when it most definitely wasn't.)

☆

Over the weekend Ugenia did lots more exciting things with her new friends, who always said nice things to her.

On Saturday Ugenia had lunch with Cara and Billy, who had brought round their new scooters for Ugenia to borrow.

They were playing outside when the phone rang.

'Ugenia, it's Bronte for you!' shouted Ugenia's dad, coming out into the garden.

'I'm busy with Cara and Billy right now. I'll call her later!' shouted Ugenia.

On Saturday evening Rudy – Ugenia's very best friend – rang her.

'Hi, Professor Lavender, is Ugenia there?'

'I'm sorry, Rudy,' said Professor Lavender, 'but she's over at Anoushka's house having a sleepover.'

'Really?' frowned Rudy. 'That's strange – she must have forgotten that it's my birthday and she was meant to be at *my* house. My mum's cooked her favourite coconut curry.'

'I'm so sorry, Rudy, I'll get her to call you later.'

On Sunday morning there was a knock at the door of 13 Cromer Road. It was Crazy Trevor.

'Hi, Mrs Lavender,' said Crazy Trevor.

'Do call me Pandora, Trevor,' said Pandora.

'Er, OK, Pandora, is Ugenia here?'

'I'm sorry, Trevor. She's out playing croquet . . . with Sebastian.'

'Croquet? What's croquet? She's meant to be playing football with me!' said Crazy Trevor, frowning.

'Oh dear, she must have forgotten. I'll get her to call you later.'

On Sunday evening Ugenia did not call Rudy, Bronte or Trevor back. She was too busy planning her diary for the coming week.

Wow, it feels so good to be so popular at last, thought Ugenia, looking at her fun-packed diary.

Monday ∞ Tennis Club with Sita
Tuesday ∞ Trampolining with Max
Wednesday ∞ Computer Club
Thursday ∞ Synchronized swimming
        with Anoushka and Chantelle
Friday ∞ Visit to Sebastian's mum's
        beauty salon for free pedicure

I'd better have an early night so I'm ready for my big week, thought Ugenia, I need my beauty sleep!

☆

On Monday morning Ugenia did such a gigantic leap out of bed that she almost smacked her head on the ceiling. She shimmied to the bathroom and gave her most ginormous toothpaste-advert smile into the mirror. 'Looking great, feeling great!' smiled Ugenia, hopping into her clothes, ready for some more of the previous week's popularity.

Ugenia arrived at the school gates ready for her big entrance.

To her confusion there were no warm smiles and no friendly comments – only sniggers and giggles. 'That's weird! What's wrong with everyone?' she muttered, frowning. Then Ugenia saw Bronte with a very worried look on her face.

As Ugenia entered the school playground, she saw, to her horror, in big white letters painted on the wall . . .

99

'INJUSTICE!!!!!!' screamed Ugenia. 'That's not true!'

'Don't worry, nits only live in clean hair,' said Bronte reassuringly.

'But I DON'T HAVE NITS, thank you very much!' snapped Ugenia. 'Who's the rotter who'd write such a thing?'

'Look, let's ignore it. Everyone will have forgotten it by lunchtime,' replied Bronte gently.

Lunchtime came and Ugenia queued up in the usual way.

'There's Miss Nit!' sniggered a girl in front of her.

'Don't stand too close,' giggled the boy behind her.

Ugenia moved on quickly and tried to pretend it wasn't happening.

After school, Ugenia went to meet Sita at Tennis Club.

'Sorry, Ugenia, but Paris is being my partner today,' said Sita. 'I forgot I asked her first.'

'OK, no problem,' said Ugenia, who felt a bit miffed. And she walked slowly back to 13 Cromer Road in a very bad mood. 'Oh well, tomorrow will be better . . . I've got trampolining with Max,' Ugenia said, trying to make herself feel better.

☆

On Tuesday morning Ugenia did a big leap out of bed. She skipped to the bathroom and gave her big toothpaste-advert smile into the mirror. 'Looking good, feeling good!' she said smiling and hopping into her clothes, ready for some more of the previous week's popularity.

Ugenia arrived at the school gates ready for a new day.

To her annoyance there were still no warm smiles, no friendly comments – only sniggers and giggles. 'What's wrong with everyone?' frowned Ugenia – and then she saw Bronte with a very worried look on her face.

To Ugenia's relief, as she entered the school playground she saw that the big white painted letters on the wall had been removed.

But to her horror, as she approached the girls' changing room she saw that written on the wall in big white painted letters was . . .

UGENIA LAVENDER SMELLS!

'INJUSTICE!!!!!!!!!' screamed Ugenia. 'That's not true!'

'Don't worry, I can't smell anything from here,' Bronte said reassuringly.

'I DON'T SMELL, thank you very much! I washed this morning!' snapped Ugenia. Who's the rotter who'd write such a thing?'

'Look, let's ignore it. Everyone will have forgotten it by lunchtime,' soothed Bronte gently.

Lunchtime came and Ugenia queued up in the usual way.

'There's Smelly Lavender!'

'Phew, what's that pong?'

'Ugenia Stink Bomb!'

'Don't stand too close,' giggled the boy behind her in the queue.

Ugenia moved on quickly and tried to pretend it wasn't happening.

After school, Ugenia went to meet Max for the trampoline party.

'Sorry, Ugenia, but there isn't any room in the minibus,' said Max. 'I forgot I asked Lindsay before you.'

'OK, no problem,' said Ugenia, who felt very miffed and walked slowly back to 13 Cromer Road in a very, very bad mood.

'Ah, Ugenia,' said her dad when she got home. 'You had a phone call – I took a message. It's on the notepad.'

MESSAGE FROM ANOUSHKA.
THURSDAY – SYNCHRONIZED SWIMMING – CAN'T MAKE IT. SORRY, I HAVE OTHER PLANS.

'Injustice!' cried Ugenia. 'This really isn't on. I thought I was popular! Well, at least tomorrow I'm launching the new Computer Club premises . . . now that is a real statement of popularity.' And Ugenia smiled, trying to make herself feel better.

☆

On Wednesday morning Ugenia did a moderate leap out of bed. She walked to the bathroom and gave an average toothpaste-advert smile into the mirror.

'Looking OK, feeling OKish!' said Ugenia, putting her clothes on, sort of ready for some more of last week's popularity.

Ugenia arrived at the school gates a little apprehensive about the day ahead.

To her distress there were still no warm smiles, no friendly comments – only sniggers and giggles. 'What's wrong with me?' frowned Ugenia. But to her relief she saw Bronte without a worried look on her face, and that the painted white letters had been removed from the girls' changing room.

Ugenia tried to forget about it all and went about the day in her usual way.

At lunchtime Ugenia hoovered up her shepherd's pie and rhubarb and custard as fast as humanly possible and went straight to the new computer room.

But as she approached the room she saw Bronte with a very concerned look on her

face. To Ugenia's horror, there in massive
white painted letters on the wall outside
was . . .

UGENIA LAVENDER, WHO DO U THINK U R?

'INJUSTICE!!!' screamed Ugenia. 'WHO
DO I THINK I AM? WHAT IS THAT
SUPPOSED TO MEAN?'

'Don't worry, it doesn't mean anything,'
said Bronte. But before they had time
to discuss it any further, Billy from the
Computer Club came over and said, 'Ah,
Ugenia, there's been a mistake. Actually,
Brittany is doing the press launch.'

'What?? But – but . . . ?' stammered
Ugenia. 'But I thought she wasn't popular
at all.'

'I'm sorry,' said Billy, shutting the door
in Ugenia's face.

'Even Brittany is more popular than me!'
cried Ugenia.

'Who's the rotter who'd write such
a thing, and why is everyone being so
horrible to me?'

'Look, let's ignore it. It will be forgotten
by tomorrow,' soothed Bronte gently.

'No, it won't! Look what's happened
– I'm completely unpopular, I'm a no one,
with no friends!' cried Ugenia.

'Well, what about me? Aren't I your
friend?' shouted Bronte. 'Thanks very
much. Maybe everyone is right – UGENIA
LAVENDER, WHO *DO* YOU THINK
YOU ARE?' And with that, Bronte burst
into tears and stormed off.

Ugenia was stunned. She'd only ever heard Bronte raise her voice once before. This was serious. 'Who do I think I am? What does it mean?' cried Ugenia as she ran into the girls' toilet, locked herself into a cubicle and began to sob uncontrollably.

Suddenly Ugenia heard a sweet, familiar voice outside the door. 'Hey, don't cry. I know how you feel. One minute I was everybody's favourite too, then I wasn't, and now I am again. It's all very unsettling,' said the voice, passing a hanky under the door with the letter B embroidered on it.

'Brittany! Thanks!' Ugenia smiled, opening the toilet door and giving Brittany a hug.

Maybe my dad could help, thought Ugenia. After all, he is a professor and he is very clever and he knows pretty much everything.

☆

After school Ugenia jumped on her red bike and sped down Boxmore Hill, past the twenty-four-hour, bargain-budget, bulk-buyers' supersized supermarket and into the town centre. She went straight to the Dinosaur Museum, where her dad worked. It was an old grey building with two stone gargoyles peering down from the roof.

Ugenia wandered through the large, stone building, under the huge diplodocus skeleton, past a stegosaurus horn, down the stairs and along a dusty, dark corridor. She tiptoed quietly past three men in white

coats wearing their do-not-disturb frowns as they peered down intently at a tiny piece of what looked like a dinosaur eyelid. Ugenia knocked on her father's door, which said:

PROFESSOR
EDWARD LAVENDER
DINOSAUR CONSULTANT

— AND —

SPECIALIST IN PRETTY
MUCH EVERYTHING ELSE

'Enter!' called Professor Lavender.

'Hi, Dad,' said Ugenia, bursting in. 'I really need your help.'

'Is this about that triceratops tooth?' asked her father, giving Ugenia a kind smile.

'No,' said Ugenia. 'Some rotter keeps writing horrid things about me around the school. A couple of days ago I was really popular, but now everyone just thinks I'm a smelly girl with nits that nobody likes! So what am I going to do?'

Professor Lavender thought hard for a couple of minutes and his eyebrows nudged each other. Then, suddenly, his face brightened up.

'Ah, it's a bit like the cavemen over thirty thousand years ago. They used to draw on their cave walls to send out warning messages threatening other tribes. Another tribe would react and strike back and write its own statement – which led to a very hostile situation that could only be resolved after one side surrendered its cave so everything was sorted,' explained Professor Lavender.

At that second, like a thunderbolt of lightning, Ugenia had a brainwave.

INGENIOUS! she thought. I'll strike back and answer them all!

'Thanks, Dad, you've been a big help.'

'Great!' Professor Lavender beamed. 'Would you like to see that triceratops tooth now?'

But Ugenia didn't hear him. She was already halfway down the corridor.

Ugenia pedalled as fast as she could back up Boxmore Hill to 13 Cromer Road. She had a plan.

☆

As soon as she got home, Ugenia rang Rudy and quickly told him everything.

'Rudy, I have a plan. It's a bit of a tricky mission impossible called THE WAR OF THE WORDS,' said Ugenia in her best action-hero, Hunk Roberts voice. 'I need the best people for the job. I need dedication and loyalty. Call Trevor and Bronte right away.'

'I'm sorry, but I'm busy right now. Maybe another time,' said Rudy, who then hung up.

'Er, OK then, see you tomorrow,' said Ugenia to the sound of the dialling tone.

She stomped upstairs and pulled down her own vision board from the top of her wardrobe. She tried to think of words she could strike back with, but her mind was blank. She couldn't concentrate, she was so distracted by Rudy being too busy for her. What's wrong with Rudy? she wondered. He's never too busy for a mission impossible. Goodness, even Rudy thinks I'm too unpopular to hang out with. Some friend he is – he's just like everyone

else! thought Ugenia, and she went to bed feeling really glum.

☆

On Thursday morning Ugenia slumped out of bed and rolled to the bathroom. She looked in the mirror with not a flicker of a toothpaste-advert smile.

'Looking sad, feeling awful!' said Ugenia, slowly putting on her clothes and not at all expecting any of last week's popularity.

'What's the point? No one likes me, everyone hates me. I might as well go and eat worms,'

Ugenia grumbled as she left for school.

On the way Ugenia decided to stop off and visit Granny Betty. She could always count on her great-grandmother for support. Granny Betty would give anyone a karate chop if they did anything mean or horrid to Ugenia, as Granny Betty loved Ugenia more than anyone else in the world.

'Oh, Granny Betty, you'll never guess what—' moaned Ugenia.

'Hmm, let me see . . . you're not as popular as last week?' interrupted Granny Betty.

'How did you know?' asked Ugenia, forgetting Granny Betty's psychic abilities.

'Well, the writing's on the wall, Ugenia. Popularity is like English weather – very unpredictable. It's hot, then cold, and it

always changes. It's what YOU think of
yourself that's important.'

'You're right, Gran,' said Ugenia,
thinking hard. 'Maybe I was so busy
thinking about what all my new friends
thought of me, I did forget what's
important.'

And with that, Ugenia marched off to
school, determined not to be bothered by
what was written about her and just be
happy within herself. In fact, she was going
to share her new wisdom with her real best
mates, Rudy, Crazy Trevor and Bronte.

Ugenia went through her usual school
day and chose to ignore all the sniggers and
chuckles.

'Whatever! Popular, schmopular!'
laughed Ugenia. 'It's what *I* think of me

that counts, right?' She wished she could tell Rudy, Bronte and Trevor what she'd discovered, but although she saw them in class they always seemed too busy to talk.

At the end of the day Ugenia went home peacefully. As she approached 13 Cromer Road, she saw a figure cycling away from her house with what looked like a tin of paint in their hands. Then she saw Bronte with a worried look on her face and, to Ugenia's horror, there on her garden wall in big white painted letters was . . .

UGENIA LAVENDER IS A . . .

'Is a what?' shouted Ugenia, and she decided to chase whoever the rotter was that had been writing it.

Ugenia sped up the road and across the green, only to find Rudy locking his bike up.

'Rudy, I'm so glad to see you! Did you see who was writing those words on my garden wall?' puffed Ugenia, who was now out of breath.

'I don't know what they were going to say though. They only managed to write Ugenia Lavender is a . . . ? I wonder what, Rudy?'

'Is a TERRIBLE FRIEND?' said Rudy.

122

Ugenia suddenly noticed little specks of white paint all over his fingers.

'Rudy? It was you all along, wasn't it? You're the rotter who's been doing all this! How could you?' cried Ugenia.

'OK, yes, I admit it. I'm the rotter and I know it was a rotten thing to do, but I felt really hurt when you missed my birthday last Saturday, and I thought that if you weren't so popular you'd want to be my best friend again and hang out with me.' Suddenly Rudy was feeling a bit silly.

'Wow, you like me so much that you went to all that trouble?' said Ugenia, smiling.

'Well, perhaps I took it a bit too far,' giggled Rudy.

'Oh, Rudy, you're the bestest friend in the whole world ever!' declared Ugenia, giving

Rudy such a massive hug his ribs hurt.

'Come back to mine for some tarberry juice to celebrate?' asked Rudy.

'I would love to! Ask Bronte and Trevor over too!' cried Ugenia excitedly – and then she stopped suddenly. 'Whoops, I've done it again,' she gulped. 'I've made other plans. I'm having tea with a new friend I've made. It's Brittany. She's really nice,' she said excitedly, 'and besides, she's just become very, very popular again!' beamed Ugenia.

uGenia Lavender

Big News!

Hello!
I know what you're thinking
– 'There she goes again, getting
herself in a pickle being a big-
head'! It's sort of true (but don't
tell anyone).

But it's strange – every time I
get a little too big for my boots,

something happens to bring me back down to earth. Yeah, I admit I was so enjoying the attention and the nice comments and being the popular one. It really made me feel good. But now I realize I must keep my feet on the ground and remember what's important.

And what about Rudy? The secret rotter! I would never have guessed in a million years! Well, I suppose we all have our moments when we freak out a bit. I think he just felt rather left out, that's all. Sometimes I can get a bit swept away by everything and that's when things go wrong.

Granny Betty knew I wasn't going to stay popular for long and that then I'd come crashing down. I suppose old people have seen it all before because they've lived so long.

Rudy, Bronte, Trevor and I have decided we are going to have a special day out and really have some fun. We haven't decided exactly what we're going to do yet, but we're meeting tomorrow with some ideas. Let the adventure begin! It's great to have friends like them – and you!

A big squeeze from me
Ugenia Lavender XX

Ingenious Top Tip

A real friend is there through the good times and the bad

I've learned through my friendship with Rudy that both of us can be a bit rubbish sometimes. But once we get through it, it's great and we love each other even more than we did before!

Brain Squeezers

Ugenia's Secret Message

I love secret codes! And I've devised this ingenious code just for you. Look at the pictures opposite, fill in the letters and discover what my top-secret message is!

133

Ugenia's Supermarket Search

Looking for the terrible tiger in the supermarket was a truly INSPIRATIONAL idea! But it wasn't easy. In fact, when Trevor and I first arrived, the only thing we could see was food, food . . . and more food. Can you find some of the food we saw in this ingenious wordsnake? The words below go in one continuous line snaking up and down, backwards and forwards, but never diagonally.

CABBAGE

CUCUMBER

CARROT

SALAMI

SALMON

MARSHMALLOWS

MINTS

Tip! Use a pencil in case you make a mistake. Then you can just start again!

Start here

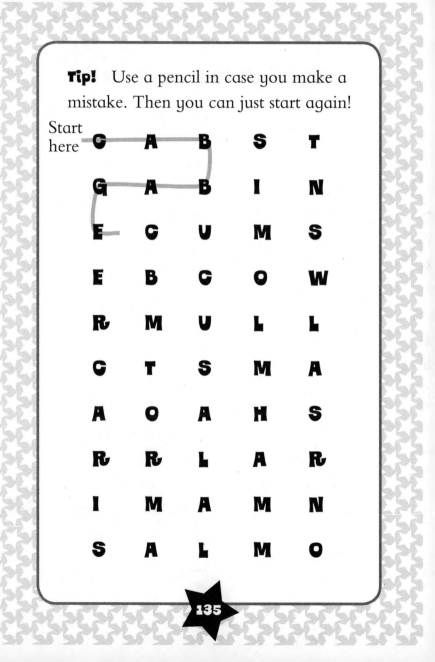

C A B S T
G A B I N
E C U M S
E B C O W
R M U L L
C T S M A
A O A H S
R R L A R
I M A M N
S A L M O

Ugenia's True or False?

A *lot* of things have been happening in my life recently. How much can you remember about them? Read the sentences below and tick either the 'TRUE' or 'FALSE' box.

1. Ugenia once dressed up as a hedge in a school play.

☐ TRUE ☐ FALSE

2. Ugenia's mum is a TV actress.

☐ TRUE ☐ FALSE

3. Lara Slater, the Leading Lady Thief, lost her voice because she had a bad cold.

☐ TRUE ☐ FALSE

4. It was Rudy who wrote those horrible things (like, 'Ugenia Lavender smells!') on the changing-room wall.

☐ TRUE ☐ FALSE

Answers

Ugenia's Secret Message
Will you be my new best friend?

Ugenia's Supermarket Search

```
C A B S T
G A B I N
E G U M S
E B O O W
R M U L L
C T S M A
A O A H S
R R I A R
I M A M N
S A L M O
```

Ugenia's True or False?

1. FALSE, but Lara thinks that would be a good part for her!

2. FALSE. She is a TV *presenter*.

3. FALSE. Lara lost her voice because she was being a diva and shouting at everyone!

4. TRUE. It *was* Rudy! Though he meant well and they're now the best of friends again.

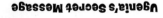

Ugenia Lavender is moving to 13 Cromer
Road. How will she fit in as the new girl
at school? Does she ever discover the
meaning of the Lovely Illness? And can
she rescue celebrity chef Uncle Harry from
a big mix-up?

UGenia Lavender

Lavender

and the Burning Pants

The school sports day is fast approaching and everyone wants to win a trophy. But then Ugenia Lavender's birthday falls on Friday the thirteenth, and things start to go from bad to worse. Will a pair of burning pants help Ugenia stop her best friend's mum from marrying the wrong person? And can Ugenia show her friends that it's the taking part that counts, but still end up with a prize?

Home Alone

Ugenia Lavender is off on holiday. What's it like being stranded on a desert island? Will she get back from holiday in time to ride the scariest ride ever at the Lunar Park Funfair? And just how will she get back to school in one piece? That depends on what happens when Ugenia is left Home Alone . . .

UGenia Lavender

Lavender

and the Temple of Gloom

Ugenia is convinced there is a real live giant
living next door to her Granny Betty. But
just how does she prove it? And can she
stop her parents from being taken in by a
beautiful bloodsucker? Just as Ugenia thinks
it can't get any worse she finds herself stuck
in the Temple of Gloom. Will she ever find a
way out?

Ugenia Lavender
The One and Only

Ugenia Lavender has discovered that the
planet is fast running out of energy. But
luckily she has a plan to save the day. How
can she help an alien return to outer space?
And what happens when she meets her
hero, Hunk Roberts? Does it make up for
the fact that Ugenia might no longer be the
One and Only?

Collect all 6
**uGenia
Lavender**
books!

Geri Halliwell

**uGenia
Lavender**

She's totally ingenious!

Got it! ☐

Geri Halliwell

**uGenia
Lavender**
and the Terrible Tiger

Got it! ☐

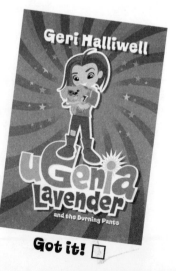

Geri Halliwell

**uGenia
Lavender**
and the Burning Pants

Got it! ☐

Got it! ☐

Geri Halliwell

uGenia Lavender and the Temple of Gloom

Got it! ☐

Got it! ☐

Log on to
ugenialavender
.com
for ingenious fun!

**Enter the world of
Ugenia Lavender and get ready
for a whole lot of fun!**

**You can find out more about the Ugenia
Lavender series plus play ingenious
games, watch fun videos and
download buddy icons and more.**

Collect all six books and get a FREE Ugenia Photo Frame!

UGENIA LAVENDER

Photo frame supplied without Geri's photo

There is a token in each Ugenia Lavender book – collect all six tokens and you can get your very own, totally free UGENIA LAVENDER photo frame!

Send your six tokens, along with your name, address and parent/guardian's signature (you must get your parent/guardian's signature to take part in this offer) to: Ugenia Lavender Photo Frame Offer, Marketing Dept, Macmillan Children's Books, The Macmillan Building, 4 Crinan Street, London N1 9XW

Ugenia Lavender Photo Frame Offer

Token 2

Collect all six tokens and get your free photo frame
Valid until 31/01/09

A selected list of titles available from Macmillan Children's Books

The prices shown below are correct at the time of going to press. However, Macmillan Publishers reserves the right to show new retail prices on covers, which may differ from those previously advertised.

All Pan Macmillan titles can be ordered from our website, www.panmacmillan.com, or from your local bookshop and are also available by post from:

Bookpost, PO Box 29, Douglas, Isle of Man IM99 1BQ
Credit cards accepted. For details:
Telephone: 01624 677237
Fax: 01624 670923
Email: bookshop@enterprise.net
www.bookpost.co.uk

Free postage and packing in the United Kingdom